# HELPING YOUR BRAND-NEW READER

**Here's how to make first-time reading easy and fun:**

▶ Read the introduction at the beginning of each story aloud. Look through the pictures together so that your child can see what happens in the story before reading the words.

▶ Read the first page to your child, placing your finger under each word.

▶ Let your child touch the words and read the rest of the story. Give him or her time to figure out each new word.

▶ If your child gets stuck on a word, you might say, *"Try something. Look at the picture. What would make sense?"*

▶ If your child is still stuck, supply the right word. This will allow him or her to continue to read and enjoy the story. You might say, *"Could this word be 'ball'?"*

▶ Always praise your child. Praise what he or she reads correctly, and praise good tries too.

▶ Give your child lots of chances to read the story again and again. The more your child reads, the more confident he or she will become.

▶ Have fun!

First edition 2002

Library of Congress Cataloging-in-Publication Data

Hurwitz, Johanna.
Ethan out and about / Johanna Hurwitz ;
illustrated by Brian Floca. —1st ed.
p.   cm. — (Brand new readers)
Summary: In four brief stories, Ethan feeds birds, squirrels,
and ants, chases a cat, and rides bikes with his Dad.
ISBN 0-7636-1098-4
[1. Animals — Fiction.  2. Food — Fiction.]
I. Floca, Brian, ill.  II. Title.  III. Series.
PZ7.H9574 Et 2002
[E] — dc21    00-037966

2 4 6 8 10 9 7 5 3 1

Printed in Hong Kong

This book was typeset in Letraset Arta.
The illustrations were done in
watercolor and ink.

Candlewick Press
2067 Massachusetts Avenue
Cambridge, Massachusetts 02140

visit us at www.candlewick.com

# ETHAN
# OUT AND
# ABOUT

## CANDLEWICK PRESS
### CAMBRIDGE, MASSACHUSETTS

## Johanna Hurwitz ILLUSTRATED BY Brian Floca

# Contents

# ETHAN'S CAT

# Introduction

This story is called *Ethan's Cat.*
It's about how Ethan chases a cat and all
of the places they run. Ethan stops chasing
the cat when he is too tired. The cat is
tired, too.

Ethan holds a cat.

4

The cat runs away.

5

Ethan chases the cat.

Ethan chases the cat over a fence.

Ethan chases the cat under a bush.

8

Ethan chases the cat up a tree.

Ethan is tired.

10

The cat is tired too.

# ETHAN'S BIKE

## Introduction

This story is called *Ethan's Bike.*
It's about what happens when Ethan rides
his bike and falls off. Dad helps Ethan get
back on. When Dad falls off his bike,
Ethan helps Dad.

Ethan rides his bike.

14

Ethan falls off his bike.

15

**Ethan rides his bike again.**

16

**Ethan falls off his bike again.**

17

Dad helps Ethan ride his bike.

Dad and Ethan ride their bikes.

19

Dad falls off his bike.

Ethan helps Dad ride his bike.

# ETHAN'S BIRDS

# Introduction

This story is called *Ethan's Birds.*
It's about how Ethan fills a bird feeder,
and how squirrels eat the birdseed
instead. Ethan gives up trying to feed
the birds. He feeds the squirrels.

Ethan fills the bird feeder.

A squirrel eats the seeds.

Ethan fills the bird feeder again.

Squirrels eat the seeds.

Ethan fills the bird feeder again.

Ethan chases the squirrels.

The squirrels come back.

Ethan feeds the squirrels.

# ETHAN'S LUNCH

# Introduction

This story is called *Ethan's Lunch*.
It's about what happens when Ethan
leaves his lunch on the picnic table.
A squirrel, a bird, and some ants eat his
lunch. When Ethan returns, his lunch
is all gone.

Ethan eats lunch.

Ethan walks away.

A squirrel eats Ethan's lunch.

The squirrel runs away.

A bird eats Ethan's lunch.

The bird flies away.

39

Ants eat Ethan's lunch.

All gone!